Magic
Animal Friends

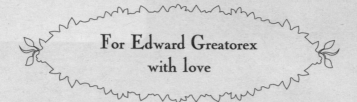

For Edward Greatorex
with love

Special thanks to Valerie Wilding

ISBN 978-0-545-94077-1

Text copyright © 2015 by Working Partners Limited
Illustrations © 2015 by Working Partners Limited

Series author: Daisy Meadows

All rights reserved. Published by Scholastic Inc., *Publishers since 1920*,
by arrangement with Working Partners Limited. Series created
by Working Partners Limited, London.

SCHOLASTIC and associated logos are trademarks and/or
registered trademarks of Scholastic Inc. MAGIC ANIMAL FRIENDS
is a trademark of Working Partners Limited.

10 9 8 7 6 5 4 3 2   16 17 18 19 20

Printed in the U.S.A.
First printing 2016

Evie Scruffypup's Big Surprise

Daisy Meadows

Scholastic Inc.

Honey Tree

Sunshine Meadow

Mr. Cleverfeather's Inventing Shed

Goldie's Grotto

Toadstool Café

Toadstool Glade

Parasol Tree

Mrs. Taptree's Library

Friendship Tree

Grizelda's Workshop

Sparkly Falls

Butterfly Bowery

Rushing Rapids

Entrance to the Caverns

Nibblesqueak Bakery

Can you keep a secret? I thought you could!

Then I'll tell you about an enchanted wood.

It lies through the door in the old oak tree,

Let's go there now—just follow me!

We'll find adventure that never ends,

And meet the Magic Animal Friends!

Love,

Goldie the Cat

Contents

CHAPTER ONE

An Autumn Visitor

Jess Forester shuffled her foot through a pile of crisp, fallen leaves. "There are lots of acorns here!" she said. She and her best friend, Lily Hart, were in Jess's yard, filling a box with fallen nuts.

"They'll be a treat for the squirrel my mom and dad are taking care of," said Lily.

The squirrel was one of the patients at Helping Paw Wildlife Hospital, which was across the street from Jess's house. Lily's parents ran it, and the two girls loved animals so much that they helped out whenever they could.

A flurry of deep gold leaves drifted down from the tree.

Jess caught one. "I love fall colors, don't you?" she said. "There's yellow and red and—look!" She pointed up through the branches. "There! A squirrel!" she said.

 2

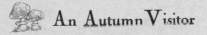

More leaves tumbled down as the
squirrel bounded higher.

"He's so sweet!" said Lily. "Maybe he'll
come to us if I offer him an acorn."

She held one out, but the squirrel stayed
on the branch, watching them nervously.

"He's shy. Let's leave
some here for him," Jess
suggested, heaping a
handful of acorns on
the grass.

"I wish we could tell
him it's safe to come
down," said Lily. "After

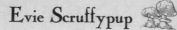

all, we've talked to squirrels before in
Friendship Forest!"

Jess grinned. Friendship Forest was a
secret world where the animals lived in
little cottages and visited the Toadstool
Café and, best of all—they talked! One
of them, a cat called Goldie, was the girls'
special friend. She had taken them on lots
of exciting adventures in the forest.

"I wish Goldie would visit us soon,"
Lily sighed.

Jess nudged her, pointing to a nearby
tree. "She's here now!" she said in delight.

A pair of green eyes, the color of grass

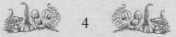

in the evening sun, blinked from between
the yellow leaves.

"Goldie!" the
girls cried.

A beautiful
golden cat
leaped from the
tree and ran to
press against
their legs, purring.

The girls bent to pet her.

"Does this mean Friendship Forest

needs our help?" wondered Lily. "Is

Grizelda causing trouble for the animals?"

Grizelda was a wicked witch. So far Jess, Lily, and Goldie had managed to stop her plans to take over the forest, but now Grizelda had four helpers—messy creatures from the Witchy Waste.

The Witchy Waste had once been a beautiful water garden, with willow trees, ponds, and waterlilies. Then Grizelda's creatures had made it as dirty as a landfill. Now she wanted them to help her make Friendship Forest messy and horrible, too, so all the animals would have to leave.

The last time Jess and Lily were in

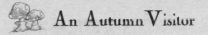

Friendship Forest, Peep the bat from
the Witchy Waste put a spell on Olivia
Nibblesqueak, a sweet little hamster. The
spell made Olivia as messy as Peep, and
had started to turn her into a bat, too!
The girls had managed to undo Peep's
spell, but they knew that three more
Witchy Waste creatures were waiting
to cause trouble.

Goldie mewed as she turned toward
the gate.

"Come on, Lily!" Jess hopped with
excitement. "Goldie's taking us to
Friendship Forest!"

 7

The girls ran down the lane, hurrying
past the wildlife hospital. Two baby
rabbits sat up inside their pen, looking
startled as the girls dashed by.

Goldie led them over the stepping-
stones in the stream at the bottom of
Lily's yard, and into Brightley Meadow.
In the middle stood an old oak tree with
bare, lifeless branches.

The Friendship Tree!

Jess and Lily shared an excited glance
as Goldie reached the tree. Something
amazing was about to happen!

Sure enough, leaves sprang from every

branch—but they weren't the bright
spring green they usually were. This
time, the leaves unfurled in glorious
autumn colors—red, yellow, orange,
and gold. They glowed in the sunshine.
Bluebirds and robins swooped down to
feast on the scarlet berries that hung from
every twig.

Goldie stretched up a paw and patted
some words carved into the tree trunk.
Jess and Lily read the words aloud:
"Friendship Forest!"

A door with a leaf-shaped handle
appeared in the trunk. Jess opened it, and

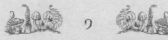

a soft golden light gleamed from inside.
Goldie slipped through the door.

The girls held hands excitedly as they
followed her into the shimmering glow.

A tingle ran right through them. Jess
and Lily knew that meant they were
shrinking, just a little.

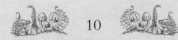

As the light faded, they found themselves in a clearing in Friendship Forest. It was always summer in the forest, and today the warm air was sweet with the popcorn scent of nearby butterpuff bushes. Little cottages were tucked among the shady tree roots.

"It's wonderful to be back," Jess began, then gasped in surprise.

Every tree was covered in a glorious blanket of blossoms.

"Wow! There are so many colors," said Lily, gazing up in wonder.

"Isn't it beautiful?" said a soft voice.

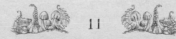

The girls spun around. Their cat friend
was standing upright, wearing her
glittering golden scarf!

"Goldie! At last we can talk to you!"
cried Lily as she ran to hug her.

"It's a very special time in Friendship
Forest," said Goldie, smiling. "Today is
Blossom Day!"

CHAPTER TWO

Blossom Day

"What's Blossom Day?" Lily asked.

"Once every year," Goldie explained, "all the trees bloom. Doesn't it look gorgeous?"

"It smells gorgeous, too!" said Jess. "Like honey and plums and jasmine all mixed together!"

"It's even better at Petal Hill," Goldie replied. "That's where we celebrate Blossom Day. Come with me!"

On the way, Jess and Lily gazed up at the dazzling petals that covered the trees.

"Those ones are so pretty!" Jess said in wonder, pointing out a cluster of purple blossoms that looked like fluffy pompoms.

Lily spotted some white flowers trailing down from the branches. "Look, they're like beautiful strings of pearls!" she said.

Soon they reached a round hill, dotted with blossom-covered shrubs.

At the foot of the hill was a rambling

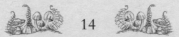

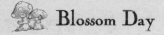

den with blue walls and a steep red roof. Yellow and white striped curtains billowed at the open windows. All around it was a garden, filled with colorful flower beds, tall trees—and lots of their animal friends!

"Hello, everyone!" called Lily and Jess. There were squeaks, quacks, and squawks of delight from the young animals.

Bella Tabbypaw the kitten hugged them, purring loudly. Molly Twinkletail the mouse and her nine brothers and sisters called ten greetings. Lola Velvetnose the mole hugged Lily's leg.

"Girls!" said Goldie.

Jess and Lily turned to see Goldie
standing with a family of dogs with thick
fluffy black-and-white fur, pointed ears,
and madly wagging tails.

"Meet Mr. and Mrs. Scruffypup," said
Goldie, "and their daughters, Evie and
Hattie."

The excited pups hugged the girls.

"Hello!" said Hattie. She was as tall as
the girls' waists and had a blue bow on
her head.

"Hello, Lily! Hello, Jess!" said Evie and

hugged both of them, her tail wagging. She had dark, sparkling eyes and was wearing pink glasses. She was smaller than her sister and her fur was much scruffier, sticking up in little tufts.

Mr. Scruffypup laughed as the pups jumped down. "We're glad to meet you, Jess and Lily," he said. "We've heard about how brave you've been, standing up to Grizelda. Come in, come in! Everyone wants to see you!"

A tiny golden hamster ran toward them, and Jess scooped her up. "Hi, Olivia Nibblesqueak!" she said.

 18

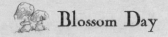

"I'm so glad you're here," the little
hamster said.

"Me, too," said Evie eagerly. "We're
going to start the blossom-drop hunt soon
and you can join in!"

"That sounds fun," said Lily, with a
laugh, "but what is the blossom-drop
hunt?"

"We have it every Blossom Day," Mrs.
Scruffypup explained. "Blossom drops are
special tasty treats—the Nibblesqueak
family makes them in their bakery, from
honeysuckle blossoms. Mr. Scruffypup
and I hide them all around Petal Hill

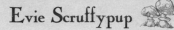

and everyone tries to find as many as they can!"

Evie bounced up and down with excitement. "Can we start the hunt now, Mom? Please?"

"Please! We can't wait!" cried the other little animals, gathering around Mr. and Mrs. Scruffypup.

Mr. Scruffpup chuckled. "We can't start just yet," he said. "We need Mr. Cleverfeather to get here first. I wonder where he could be?"

Jess gave a cry as she spotted an old owl, wearing a waistcoat and monocle,

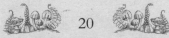

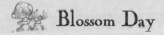

hurrying toward Petal Hill. Under one wing was tucked a machine that looked like a mini vacuum cleaner. "Here he comes!" she said.

"Lorry I'm sate," panted the owl as he reached them, mixing up his words like he always did. "I mean, sorry I'm late. I've got my Peffal Putter," he said, patting the machine, "so we can start the hunt!"

 21

"He means Petal Puffer," Goldie whispered to the girls with a grin.

"Thank you, Mr. Cleverfeather," said Mrs. Scruffypup. "Now when the Petal Puffer puffs, the hunt for the blossom drops begins!"

Lily, Jess, Goldie, and the little animals lined up excitedly in front of Mr. Cleverfeather. Evie was holding on to her big sister's paw, her tail wagging with excitement.

"Petals ready! Puffer steady! Go!" Mr. Cleverfeather hooted.

He pressed a button and the Puffer

whooshed thousands of petals high up above them. They drifted slowly downward like colorful confetti. With squeals of delight, the animals ran off to hunt for blossom drops. Lola Velvetnose and Olivia Nibblesqueak ran into the den, while Bella Tabbypaw darted over to search in a flower bed.

"Look!" Bella cried, holding up a little package made of leaves. "I've found some blossom drops!"

"Let's search in the tree house," said Hattie. "It's this way!"

The girls and Goldie ran after the two

puppies as they bounded over to a huge old apple tree. Built all around the trunk, and reaching up into the branches, was the most amazing wooden tree house they'd ever seen.

"Wow!" gasped Jess as she stared up at the different levels. There were curtains at the windows and pretty flowers painted all around the door.

"Dad made it,"
said Evie. "Me and
Hattie have lots of fun
in here. Let's see if
there are any blossom
drops inside!"

Evie and Hattie climbed
into the tree house. Then
they vanished from sight!

"Where are you?" Lily
called up to them.

"Surprise!" Evie giggled,
popping up at a third-
floor window.

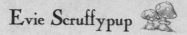

"Hi!" cried Hattie, looking out a door on the second level.

Evie disappeared for a moment, then leaned out of the topmost window. "Boo!"

Laughing, the girls and Goldie followed them inside. More flowers were painted on the walls, and they went up a wooden ladder to the next level, where Evie and Hattie were searching through a huge pile of toys.

Evie give a *yip* of excitement, and from inside a box of wooden animals she pulled out a small packet made of leaves tied with grass strands.

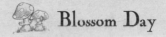
"Surprise!" Evie called. "Blossom drops!"

She handed the package to Lily, who opened it. Inside were lots of oval, honeysuckle-scented treats.

"Mmm!" Lily said as she ate one. "It's gooey in the middle! That was a surprise."

Evie giggled and Hattie pulled her into a hug. "Evie loves surprises!" Hattie said, ruffling her little sister's fluffy fur.

They all jumped when they heard a terrified squeal.

"Eeeeeeeck!"

It came from the Scruffypups' den.

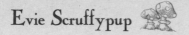

"What was that?" asked Goldie, her tail twitching with worry.

They hurried out of the tree house. Little animals were bursting out the front door of the den, scurrying to their parents. The girls and Goldie ran over. Through the windows, they could see a rat, a crow, a toad, and a bat charging through the den, chasing the frightened animals.

"The creatures from the Witchy Waste!" cried Lily. "They're stealing all the blossom drops!"

CHAPTER THREE

Masha's Spell

"Come on!" cried Lily as she, Jess, and Goldie ran into the den.

The Witchy Waste creatures were hurtling around the Scruffypups' kitchen. Snippit the crow flapped his tattered wings at Lola Velvetnose the mole. She'd dropped her big purple-framed glasses

and didn't see him
until he was right next
to her. She shrieked and
knocked over some
saucepans. "This way,
Lola!" called Goldie,
helping her to the door.
Masha the rat waved
her straw hat as she pushed the kitchen

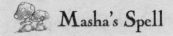

chairs over. "Yee-ha!" she cried. "This
is fun!"

Lily scooped Olivia Nibblesqueak
out of the teacup she was hiding inside.
"You're safe now," she told the tiny
hamster, as she carried her outside and
placed her on the grass.

"Stop it! You're scaring everyone!" Jess
shouted.

Hopper the toad crawled out from under
the kitchen table. She poked her wide,
flat tongue out at Jess.
Peep the bat landed
on a shelf, giggling

as he sent a stack of plates crashing to the floor. "Lovely mess!" he squeaked.

There were frightened cries from outside the den. Through the window, the girls saw a familiar yellow-green orb floating over Petal Hill.

"Oh, no!" groaned Lily, as they ran back out of the den.

Cra-ack! The orb burst into smelly yellow-green sparks.

Mr. Cleverfeather flapped backward as the sparks cleared, revealing Grizelda in her purple tunic. Her skinny black pants were tucked into shiny boots with thin high heels. The witch's green hair hung around her shoulders like wet seaweed as she threw back her head, cackling.

"It's the meddling girls and the interfering cat," Grizelda said. "You might have stopped Peep's fun, but Masha, Snippit, and Hopper haven't cast their spells yet." Her dark eyes glittered as she pointed at the watching animals with a bony finger. "Soon Masha will use her magic on one of you—then you'll turn into a messy rat, too!"

Jess, Lily, and Goldie stood their ground as the animals ran and hid, squealing.

Grizelda laughed. "The spell will make whoever it touches love messiness as much as Masha and her friends. Soon, the forest will be filled with creatures who love messiness and dirt! Friendship Forest will become so filthy that all you silly animals will have to leave. Ha-haa!"

Jess shouted bravely, "You won't win!"

"We'll see about that!" Grizelda

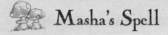

snapped her fingers and disappeared in a
burst of spitting sparks.

The animals were staring at each other
in horror. A flash of movement caught
Lily's eye—Masha the rat was scuttling
toward Evie!

"Look out!" Lily yelled.

But Masha had already reached the
little puppy. She turned around and shook
her long pink tail. A shower of purple
sparks cascaded over Evie.

Goldie's paws flew to her mouth. "Oh,
no!" she cried.

Evie shook her fluffy fur. She sat still

for a moment, but she looked exactly the same as she had before.

"Maybe nothing will happen," said Jess hopefully.

But then Evie gave a *yip*. She darted to Bella Tabbypaw, snatched her blossom drop package, and threw the sweets all over the ground. "Look, a nice mess!" she cried.

"Oh, no," said Goldie, "poor Evie already thinks she's a messy rat!"

"Hee-hee!" giggled Masha. "Let's take them all!" Evie and the Witchy Waste creatures ran into the trees, taking the rest of the stolen blossom drops with them.

"Come back!" called Mr. Scruffypup.

But Evie had disappeared into the forest.

Evie's mom gave a horrified cry and grasped the girls' hands in her paws. "What shall we do?"

Jess hugged her. "Don't worry," she said, "We'll get Evie back."

"We helped Olivia Nibblesqueak, remember?" said Lily, putting an arm around Hattie.

"That's right," said Goldie. "We found a spell in Mrs. Taptree's library when Olivia started behaving like a bat. It stopped the messy magic before and it can do it again!"

Jess reached into her pocket and pulled out the mini-sketchbook she always carried with her.

"I copied it down," she said, flipping

 38

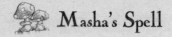

through the pages. "Listen—it's a spell to turn you back to your normal self.

You want to be yourself again?

Then here's what you must do.

Gather up those favorite things

That mean the most to you.

What do you like to do the most?

What food do you love the best?

And what is your biggest secret?

Now here's a little test.

Put them in your favorite place,

The place you love to be.

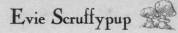

If someone names those things aloud,
Yourself once more you'll be.

Hattie Scruffypup's face brightened. "So we need to find Evie's favorite things?"

"Exactly!" Lily beamed. "If we do that, we can save her!"

 40

CHAPTER FOUR

Ellie's Surprise

Mrs. Scruffypup dabbed her eyes. "Let me see . . . Evie's favorite food is blossom drops," she said, her eyes filling with tears. "But those horrible Witchy Waste creatures have taken them all."

"Don't cry," Lily said. "Maybe the Nibblesqueaks will make some more."

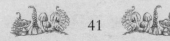

"Of course we will!" Olivia said. "But we'll need lots more honeysuckle. It takes twenty blossoms to make one single blossom drop."

Mr. Scruffypup's ears pricked up. "Follow me," he said. "I know where we can find some!"

Goldie, the girls, and all the other animals followed him around Petal Hill to a tall tree. It was covered in curling stems of honeysuckle, but all the flowers on the lower branches had been picked. The rest were too high to reach, even for the girls.

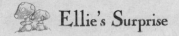

"Oh, no! How can we get those flowers?" asked Jess.

"I know!" cried Lily. "Mr. Cleverfeather, can you use your Petal Puffer to blow them off?"

"Of course!" the owl said. "Anything to help little Evie Puffyscrup!"

He aimed the Puffer upward and pressed the button.

Shoo-woosh!

Honeysuckle flowers blew into the air and showered down.

All the animals hurried around gathering the flowers, and the girls soon

had arms full of blossoms. It was like holding a soft, scented cloud.

Hattie bounded over, clutching a little basket. Lily and Jess filled it up to the brim with flowers.

"Olivia's too little to carry the basket," Hattie said, "so I'll take it back to the bakery for her."

She and Olivia ran off into the trees.

"That's Evie's favorite food

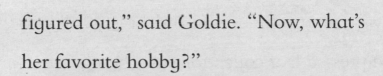

figured out," said Goldie. "Now, what's her favorite hobby?"

"Collecting things!" said Mrs. Scruffypup. "Evie's bedroom's full of her collections. Come and see."

They went back to the Scruffypups' den, and Mr. and Mrs. Scruffypup led them upstairs to a pretty pink bedroom. The shelves and a little desk were crammed

with pretty things. On the windowsill was
a pressed leaf collection, and beside the
bed was a pile of acorns. Hanging from
the ceiling was a collection of nuts, which
were strung together on grass stalks.

Goldie gazed around the room. "These
are wonderful," she said. "But which is
Evie's favorite?"

Mrs. Scruffypup's face lit up. "That's
easy!" she exclaimed.

She crouched down, lifted the edge of
Evie's frilled quilt cover and felt around
beneath the bed. After a few moments, she
stood up again.

"That's funny," Mrs. Scruffypup said. She looked around with a puzzled expression. "Evie's favorite is her jewel collection. She keeps it in a little woven basket under her bed, but it's gone. Maybe she left it behind the last time she went to get more jewels?"

Mr. Scruffypup gave a *yap* of worry. "If we can't find Evie's favorite collection, Goldie and the girls can't help her."

 47

"We won't give up," Lily said
determinedly. "Where does Evie go to find
the jewels?"

"The cavern beneath Toadstool Glade, I
think," Mrs. Scruffypup said.

"Of course!" said Jess. "It's got jewels
on the ceiling! We saw them during our
adventure with Bella Tabbypaw. Don't
worry, we'll save Evie!"

Lily, Jess, and Goldie hurried from Petal
Hill, making their way through the forest
toward Toadstool Glade.

On the way, they passed the Treasure
Tree, where the forest animals got all the

food they needed.
A tiny pair of red
boots stood at the
bottom.

"Quack, quack,
quack!" said an
unhappy voice
above them. Ellie
Featherbill the
duckling swung
down on one of the
ropes that dangled
from the tree.

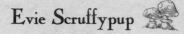

"Hello, Ellie!" said Lily. "What's the matter?"

The duckling hugged the girls. "I came to get blackberries for Mom to make a pie," she explained, "but they're all gone!"

Jess held Ellie's wingtip to help her balance while she put her boots on.

Ellie put one foot in.

Squelch!

"Yuck!' she said, and her feathers quivered. She pulled her foot out. It was covered in squished blackberry. "Yucky!" she quacked, and jumped up and down, trying to shake the mess off.

The girls peered inside Ellie's boots.

They were full of blackberries!

"That was a nasty surprise!" said Jess.

"You poor thing!"

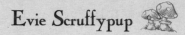

Ellie looked upset. "Who would be horrible enough to do that?"

The girls and Goldie shared a glance.

"Evie loves surprises, doesn't she?" said Lily. "It must be her and Masha!"

CHAPTER FIVE

The Jewel Cavern

Lily gently wiped the duckling's foot with velvety moss while Jess explained what had happened to Evie.

"So Evie didn't mean to be unkind," Jess said. "She just can't help it at the moment. Masha's spell is making her love messes— and messy surprises!"

Goldie came over with her paws full
of raspberries. She popped them in Ellie's
basket. "There aren't any blackberries left,
but these will make a nice pie," she said.

Ellie's eyes sparkled. "Thanks, Goldie!"
she quacked.

The girls and Goldie hugged the
duckling good-bye, then hurried through
the forest.

After a while, Goldie stopped and held
up a paw. "Something's moving up ahead,"
she said. "Maybe it's Evie and Masha."

They heard a sharp giggle. "Hee-hee!"

Goldie whirled around, her ears

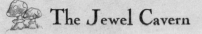

pricked. "I can't tell where it's coming from," she said.

"Perhaps that sneaky pair are following us," suggested Lily.

"Let's not worry about them for now," said Jess. "We need that jewel collection. Come on!"

They hurried on and finally emerged from the trees near the entrance to one of the tunnels leading to the cavern.

Lily jumped as a twig snapped, right above her head. She looked up.

"Evie and Masha!" she cried. "So they *were* following us!"

The little black-and-white puppy shouted, "Surprise!" and threw a big pawful of blackberries at Lily.

"Stop!" Jess cried, but the only reply she got was a splatter of juicy ripe berries in her curly blond hair.

Evie laughed as Masha threw more blackberries. They splattered against the trees, covering the bark in sticky juice.

"Hee! What a lovely mess!" said Masha. She hurried off, Evie following after her— but instead of bounding as she usually

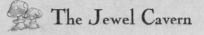

did, Evie scuttled with her body close to the ground.

"She's behaving just like a rat!" said Lily with a groan.

Jess nodded. "We have to lift Masha's spell before she turns into a rat for good. Come on, let's hurry!"

They quickly cleaned off the purple blackberry mush as best they could, then

 went into the tunnel. It wasn't as dark as it was the last time they were there, when they went to rescue Bella Tabbypaw.

"Mr. Fuzzybrush the fox dug holes in the tunnel roof so the sun can shine in and light the way," said Goldie. "Now all the animals can come and see the jewels."

"Look, Jess!" said Lily, as they approached the huge cavern. "I'd forgotten how big it was."

Jess gazed in awe at the cavern roof, which was studded with brilliantly glittering jewels of every color.

"How does little Evie manage to reach them?" Jess wondered.

"She doesn't need to," Goldie smiled. "Look down."

The girls gasped. Now the cavern was lighter, they saw something they'd never noticed before. The floor of the cave was dotted with beautiful jewels, too!

"Wow!" said Jess.

"There are so many!" Lily said, gazing at the glittering stones.

"We have to find Evie's collection,"

said Jess. "Remember, she kept it in a woven basket. Let's look."

Lily searched a pile of fallen rocks, while Jess looked in all the nooks and crevices along the far wall. Goldie searched behind the great columns that supported the roof.

They'd only been looking for a few minutes when Jess heard Lily cry, "I found it! And something else, too."

Goldie and Jess ran to see.

The little basket had fallen on its side, spilling out colorful jewels.

"Look at Evie's wonderful collection!"

said Goldie. "They're all different shapes—round ones, square ones . . ."

"Even a heart-shaped one," said Jess, as she piled the jewels back into the basket.

"Look," said Lily. She picked up some string lying close by. "Evie must have been making something."

A few paces away, they found a neat pile of golden leaves and golden twigs.

"What was Evie making?" Jess wondered. "We'd better hang on to them—we might need them for our spell."

Several tunnels led out of the cavern. They couldn't decide which one to take

 61

until Lily noticed something on the floor at one of the entrances. A golden leaf. Just a little farther on was another one.

"Evie must have dropped them," said Jess. "You know what this means? We can follow her trail! We know what her favorite food is and her favorite hobby— it might help us find out her secret."

Goldie set off. "Let's hurry," she called back. "Evie was already acting so much like Masha, there can't be much time left. If we don't break the spell, she'll turn into a messy rat for good!"

CHAPTER SIX

Mud Pies

The trail of golden leaves led the friends through the tunnel. They came out near Willowtree River.

A tree with delicate trailing branches and golden leaves stood on the riverbank. "So that's where Evie got the leaves from," said Jess, pointing.

Perched up in the tree, where the trunk divided into five branches, was a tiny little cottage.

"It's so pretty," said Lily, looking closer at the willow twig walls and the braided reed roof.

The door opened, and out popped a kingfisher! Her beak opened in surprise.

"Jess and Lily!" she said. "And Goldie, too!"

It was Mrs. Blueflash! She and her family had helped the girls in their adventures before.

"Chicks!" the kingfisher called, and the

whole family flew out to flutter around
the girls' heads, blowing kisses with their
wingtips.

"Mrs. Blueflash, we need help," said Jess.
She explained about Evie and her pile of
golden leaves.

"Evie has a special secret," said Lily.
"We have to discover what it is, otherwise

she'll turn into a rat like Masha from the
Witchy Waste. Do you know anything
about it?"

"All I know is that Evie wanted some
of our golden leaves for a surprise present
she's making," Mrs. Blueflash said.

"What is it?" Goldie asked.

"Who's it for?" asked Jess.

Mrs. Blueflash shook her head. "I'm
afraid I don't know."

Splat!

"Ow!" cried Lily. A big, sloppy ball of
mud had hit her on the arm. "Oh, yuck.
Who threw—"

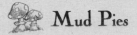

Splat!

More mud hit the Blueflashes' cottage
and ran gloopily down the front window.

Splat!

Another sputtered all over Jess's hair.
"Ugh!" she cried. "Evie and Masha must
have followed us here!"

"There they are!" said Mrs. Blueflash,
pointing her wing across the river. "Chee-
kee! Chee-kee!" she cried.

Jess and Lily looked toward the
opposite bank. There, giggling away,
was Evie with Masha, Peep, Snippit,
and Hopper. They were bending back a

springy tree branch and loading it with
mud. When they let go of the branch,
the mud catapulted across the river.

Evie scurried to the water's edge.
"SURPRISE!" she yelled, then turned to
Masha. "We should throw mud all around
the rest of the forest, too!"

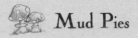

"Ooh, yes," said the rat, "then it'll be lovely and messy." She launched another mud missile.

"Oh, no," Mrs. Blueflash squawked. "Mud is very bad for feathers! Hurry, children, hide!"

"Over here!" a small voice called to the girls.

Lily and Jess turned to see the smallest kingfisher chick hiding among the leaves of a bush. They dove behind it, Lily grabbing Goldie's paw and pulling her with them.

The chick was shaking with fright, so

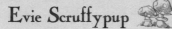

Lily carefully lifted her up and stroked her feathers soothingly.

"I'm Bethany," the chick said, her voice trembling, "and Evie's my friend. I really want her back to normal!" She gave a sob.

"Don't worry," said Jess. "We'll help her. But we have to find out about her secret present."

"I'm sorry," Bethany said sadly, wiping her eyes with a wing. "I don't know what it is." Her face brightened. "But I think I know where it's hidden!"

"That's wonderful!" said Lily. "Do you think you could show us?"

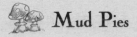

Bethany gave another tremble, but
then she puffed up her feathers. "Yes," she
said determinedly, "I'll show you. I'd do
anything to save Evie."

"Thank you!"
said Goldie,
stroking the
chick's bright
blue and orange
feathers.

"Mom, I'm going
to help Evie!" Bethany called.

"Please be careful!" Mrs. Blueflash
called back.

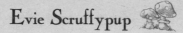

"We'll take care of her!" Jess promised. And they hurried away after Bethany, dodging the balls of mud that whizzed all around them.

CHAPTER SEVEN

A Secret in Petal Dell

Bethany led Goldie and the girls
back toward Petal Hill. Mr. and Mrs.
Scruffypup and Hattie were waiting
anxiously outside their den.

"I've got the blossom drops from
Olivia," said Hattie, holding up a full
basket. Her eyes were wide with worry.

 73

"Have you found all of Evie's favorite things yet?"

"Just one more to go," said Jess. She turned to the kingfisher chick. "Bethany's helping us!"

The kingfisher fluttered over and perched on Jess's outstretched hand. "It's this way!" she chirped.

Hattie tucked the basket over her paw. "I'm coming to help," she said. "I miss Evie so much!"

Bethany zoomed up Petal Hill. Goldie and Hattie followed, bounding easily between the blossom-laden bushes.

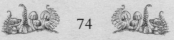

A surprise awaited them. At the top of the hill, the ground dipped into a hidden flowery dell. It was like a little sheltered valley, and the scent of jasmine hung in the warm air. The grass was soft and cushiony and in the middle was a copse of blossom-covered pear trees. Petals fluttered down as the branches swayed in the breeze.

"This is Petal Dell," said Bethany.

"Over here!" Goldie called.

The girls and Hattie ran up the slope to join her. Goldie pointed at the flowers. Most of them were yellow, but in the

 75

middle, dark blue flowers were arranged
into shapes.

"They're planted in the shapes of
letters!" Lily cried.

Hattie gasped. "They're spelling out
a word—my name! Look, they say
'Hattie'!"

Then Bethany called from the pear
trees. "Come and see!" she chirped.

Goldie and the girls ran down past the
flowers, into the trees. Bright balloons and
streamers hung from every branch.

"It's decorated for a party!" said Jess.

Lily spotted something glinting beneath

a starflower bush and picked it up. It
was a beautiful little crown, made of
golden willow leaves and decorated with
brilliant jewels.

"This must be what Evie was making,"
she said, showing the others.

Jess gave a cry. "Oh! Now I know what

the surprise is! Evie was planning a party for you, Hattie!"

Hattie clapped her paws together in delight.

"And this must be a crown she made for you," Lily smiled, placing it gently on Hattie's head.

"Blossom Day is the day before my birthday," Hattie said, her eyes shining. "I always feel a little sad because everyone's always tired after the celebrations, so my birthday doesn't feel very special. I've never told Evie, but she must have guessed!"

"And so she
decided to give you a
secret surprise party,"
said Lily.

Bethany nodded.
"Evie thinks this is the prettiest place
in the whole of Friendship Forest," she
chirped. "That must be why she decided
to have it here."

Hattie smiled. "Evie's the best little sister
a puppy could have."

"And thanks to you," Jess said, "we've
got everything we need to turn her back
into her normal puppy self." She took the

basket of blossom drops from Hattie and put it down. "Her favorite food!"

Lily added the basket of jewels. "Her favorite things."

"Her secret is the surprise party for Hattie," said Goldie, as Hattie lay down the crown, "and her favorite place is Petal Dell." Her ears pricked up. "Can you hear giggling?"

The girls listened. A moment later, they heard it, too.

"Evie and Masha must have followed us again," Lily whispered.

"They're probably planning another

 80

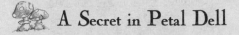

horrible, messy surprise," Jess said softly.
She drew a sharp breath. "Shhhh! They're
coming!"

Masha and Evie scurried out from the
bushes nearby.

"What's going on?" Masha demanded.
She sat up on her back legs, chattering
her teeth, and Evie did the same. Her
fluffy, scruffy coat was now as dirty as
Masha's dirty fur. Hattie gave a cry of
horror as she saw her sister.

Lily hugged Hattie. "Don't worry, we
have all of Evie's favorite things. We'll
save your sister!"

But Evie scooped up a big pawful of mud from the ground. *Squelch!* The mud splattered over her favorite things.

"That was fun!" giggled Evie, and she and Masha laughed loudly at the mess.

"She doesn't even recognize them," Jess said, her stomach twisting with worry. "What if we're too late?"

CHAPTER EIGHT

Party Time!

"We can't give up now," said Goldie. "Let's do the spell—and quickly!"

As Evie and Masha scooped up more mud, Jess chanted, "Evie's favorite hobby . . . collecting jewels!"

"Evie's favorite food," shouted Goldie. "Blossom drops!"

"Evie's secret . . . a special surprise party!" added Lily.

They joined hands and said together, "In Evie's favorite place—Petal Dell!"

Purple sparks flew from Evie. Her fluffy fur stood all on end for a moment, and then the dirt disappeared so that her white stomach was as snowy white as before. She blinked a couple of times, then her tail began to wag.

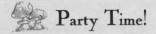

"Hooray!" cried Lily and Jess.

"Evie's herself again," Goldie said, with tears of joy in her green eyes.

For a moment, the puppy seemed confused. She looked at Masha, then at the girls, then at Hattie. Finally, she gave a *yap* and bounded over to her sister. "What happened?" she asked.

Lily ruffled the white fluff above Evie's nose. "Naughty Masha put a spell on you," she explained, "but everything's fine now."

Masha's teeth chattered angrily again. "This is no good," she grumbled. "Evie's no fun anymore."

Goldie looked at Masha sternly. "It's not nice to mess up the forest," she told the rat.

"But it's so much fun!" said Masha. Her face brightened. "I'm going to go and find my other friends so we can keep being messy!"

She scurried down Petal Hill.

Goldie sighed. "If only we could make the Witchy Waste creatures go home again," she said. "But I just can't think how."

Bethany had flown high up to watch Masha leave. She suddenly did an

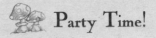

about-face and zoomed back.
"Something's coming!" she said, and
perched on Lily's shoulder, gripping
tightly with her little feet.

A yellow-green orb appeared over the
top of the hill. Lily and Jess knew what
that meant. Grizelda!

The orb burst in a shower of stinky
sparks. There stood the witch, her green
hair writhing madly. She was so angry
that her face was almost as purple as
her tunic.

Grizelda stamped her foot. "Masha
might have failed," she screeched, "but

just you wait!
Soon Snippit and
Hopper will cast
their magic on
those silly animals
and Friendship
Forest will be
mine! Ha!"

She snapped her
fingers and
disappeared in a burst of smelly sparks.

"It's over," Goldie said, putting an arm
around Hattie and Evie.

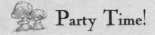

It was early evening in Petal Dell and everyone was enjoying Hattie's birthday party. Olivia and the other Nibblesqueaks had brought lots of tasty treats from their bakery. There were cheesy twists, fruit pies, honey biscuits, and three types of cake: raspberry cream sponge, lemon roll, and a birthday cake covered with Nibblesqueaks' Famous Nectar Icing. Olivia had iced *Happy Birthday, Hattie!* on it.

Hattie was wearing her birthday crown. "This is the best surprise ever, Evie," she said. "It's wonderful!"

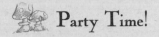

"Having your party a day early was part of the surprise," Evie said happily, as Hattie pulled her into a hug. "I'm so glad you like it!"

Mr. Cleverfeather had brought his Music-o-Matic. It was an enormous machine with a trumpet, drum, harp, and xylophone that played itself. Whenever anyone pressed a button and shouted, "All change!" a different tune played.

The Scruffypups were so delighted to have Evie back that they couldn't stop dancing. The Longwhiskers family got everyone joining in the bunny hop, while the Blueflash family flew back and forth so the setting sun's rays glinted on their orange and blue feathers.

Soon it was time for Jess and Lily to go home. Evie and Hattie hugged them good-bye.

"Thank you so much for saving me," said Evie. Her fur was even scruffier than usual because she'd been dancing so much!

"You're very welcome," said Lily, giving her another cuddle.

Everyone waved good-bye.

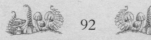

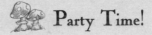

"Snippit and Hopper will cast their spells soon, won't they?" Jess said as Goldie led the girls to the Friendship Tree.

"When they do, we'll be ready to help stop them," promised Lily.

Goldie smiled and squeezed their hands with her paws. "You're the best friends we animals could wish for."

She touched the trunk and a door opened. The girls hugged Goldie and stepped into golden shimmering light. They felt the tingle that told them they were returning to their normal size and, as the light faded, they found themselves back in Brightley Meadow. The sun was still high. No time ever passed while they were in Friendship Forest!

"That was an amazing adventure," said Lily with a smile.

"I know!" Jess grinned. "I can't wait until next time."

They made their way back to Jess's yard, kicking up piles of red, yellow, and gold autumn leaves as they went. When they looked up at the tree, the little squirrel still sat on a branch, looking down at them.

Jess offered him an acorn. Both girls

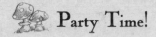

held their breath as the squirrel scampered
down the tree, paused, then hopped over
to Jess. He took the acorn and ran off
toward the garden shed.

"What's he doing?" asked Jess. "I
thought squirrels buried their acorns."

"He is burying
it," Lily giggled,
"in one of your
dad's boots!"

Jess burst out
laughing. "That'll
give Dad a
surprise!"

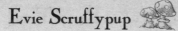

The two girls shared a smile. They knew a little puppy who loved to give surprises!

The End

Lily and Jess are back in Friendship Forest and they can't wait to spend time with little otter Chloe Slipperslide. But when Grizelda casts a spell, Chloe starts to hide all the shiny objects in Friendship Forest!

Can Lily and Jess find all of Chloe's favorite things and break the spell? Find out in the next adventure,

Chloe Slipperslide's Secret

Turn the page for a sneak peek . . .

"Run!" Goldie yelled to the animals. "Quick, before Snippit casts his spell on you!"

The crow was already ruffling his scruffy feathers, and purple sparks were flying around him. The animals fled in panic, rushing to hide in the trees and bushes.

But when Lily looked back, she was horrified to see that Chloe hadn't moved.

"Chloe! Run!" Lily cried.

But Chloe just crouched with her paws over her eyes and her long tail quivering.

"She's too scared to move," cried Jess. "I'll get her!"

But before she could reach Chloe, purple sparks splattered over the frightened little otter.

Lily gasped. "Oh, no! Snippit's put a spell on Chloe!"

Read

Chloe Slipperslide's Secret

to find out what happens next!

Puzzle Fun!

Evie Scruffypup is throwing a surprise party for her sister, Hattie!

Can you spot the differences between these two pictures?

ANSWERS

1. Mouse is missing
2. Hattie is missing her smile
3. There is an extra balloon
4. There is no pattern on the drum
5. Jess is missing a pocket

Lily and Jess's Animal Facts

Lily and Jess love lots of different animals—
both in Friendship Forest
and in the real world.

Here are their top facts about

BORDER COLLIES

like Evie Scruffypup.

- Evie Scruffypup is a breed of working dog called a border collie.

- Working dogs have been used for the last 12,000 years, mostly for herding sheep, cattle, goats, and other farm animals.

- Border collies like Evie are the most intelligent dog species in the world.

- Some border collies have learned to react to hundreds of words and whistles for all different types of jobs.

- Border collies usually have litters of six puppies.

RAINBOW magic™

Which Magical Fairies Have You Met?

- ☐ The Rainbow Fairies
- ☐ The Weather Fairies
- ☐ The Jewel Fairies
- ☐ The Pet Fairies
- ☐ The Dance Fairies
- ☐ The Music Fairies
- ☐ The Sports Fairies
- ☐ The Party Fairies
- ☐ The Ocean Fairies
- ☐ The Night Fairies
- ☐ The Magical Animal Fairies
- ☐ The Princess Fairies
- ☐ The Superstar Fairies
- ☐ The Fashion Fairies
- ☐ The Sugar & Spice Fairies
- ☐ The Earth Fairies
- ☐ The Magical Crafts Fairies
- ☐ The Baby Animal Rescue Fairies
- ☐ The Fairy Tale Fairies

■ SCHOLASTIC

Find all of your favorite fairy friends at
scholastic.com/rainbowmagic

HIT entertainment

RMFAIRY13

RAINBOW magic™

Which Magical Fairies Have You Met?

- ❏ Joy the Summer Vacation Fairy
- ❏ Holly the Christmas Fairy
- ❏ Kylie the Carnival Fairy
- ❏ Stella the Star Fairy
- ❏ Shannon the Ocean Fairy
- ❏ Trixie the Halloween Fairy
- ❏ Gabriella the Snow Kingdom Fairy
- ❏ Juliet the Valentine Fairy
- ❏ Mia the Bridesmaid Fairy
- ❏ Flora the Dress-Up Fairy
- ❏ Paige the Christmas Play Fairy
- ❏ Emma the Easter Fairy
- ❏ Cara the Camp Fairy
- ❏ Destiny the Rock Star Fairy
- ❏ Belle the Birthday Fairy

- ❏ Olympia the Games Fairy
- ❏ Selena the Sleepover Fairy
- ❏ Cheryl the Christmas Tree Fairy
- ❏ Florence the Friendship Fairy
- ❏ Lindsay the Luck Fairy
- ❏ Brianna the Tooth Fairy
- ❏ Autumn the Falling Leaves Fairy
- ❏ Keira the Movie Star Fairy
- ❏ Addison the April Fool's Day Fairy
- ❏ Bailey the Babysitter Fairy
- ❏ Natalie the Christmas Stocking Fairy
- ❏ Lila and Myla the Twins Fairies
- ❏ Chelsea the Congratulations Fairy
- ❏ Carly the School Fairy
- ❏ Angelica the Angel Fairy
- ❏ Blossom the Flower Girl Fairy

3 stories in each one!

▥ SCHOLASTIC

Find all of your favorite fairy friends at
scholastic.com/rainbowmagic

HIT entertainment

RMSPECIAL17

Visit Friendship Forest, where animals can talk and magic exists!

Meet best friends Jess and Lily and their adorable animal pals in this enchanting series from the creator of Rainbow Magic!

■SCHOLASTIC

scholastic.com

MAGICAF2